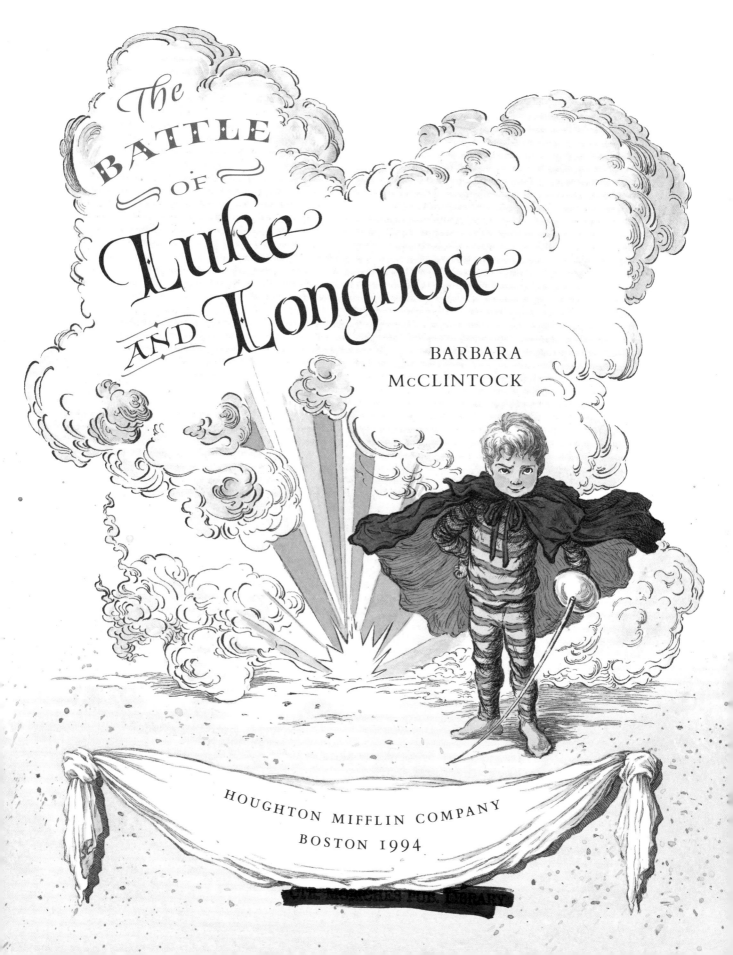

The BATTLE OF Luke AND Longnose

BARBARA McCLINTOCK

HOUGHTON MIFFLIN COMPANY

BOSTON 1994

Inspired by and lovingly dedicated to Larson

Library of Congress Cataloging-in-Publication Data

McClintock, Barbara.
  The battle of Luke and Longnose / by Barbara McClintock.
  p.   cm.
  Summary: When the soldiers in Luke's cardboard theatre come to
life, he and his cat Rags help them defeat the evil Longnose.
  ISBN 0-395-65751-2
  [1. Toys—Fiction.   2. Magic—Fiction.]   I. Title.
PZ7.M47841418Bat   1994   93-12815
[E]—dc20   CIP
                               AC

Printed in the United States of America

BP   10   9   8   7   6   5   4   3   2   1

No one can stay awake forever.

Luke had finally fallen asleep, after one last battle with the soldiers in his new theater. He slept peacefully, the night still and cool around him.

"Ka boom!" Luke jumped up in bed.

"Hey!" he cried out. "Rags, what was that! Something blew up in my theater!"

As smoke filled the room, the theater grew and grew until Luke, Rags, and the bed were tiny figures on the now gigantic stage.

"This is great! Great and wonderful!" Luke whispered to Rags.

"That was a close one!" huffed a soldier, stepping up to Luke's bed. "Captain Fearsome reporting, Sir. That infamous scalawag Longnose has escaped from jail and launched an attack on us, Sir. He vows revenge on us and wants to take control of the theater. He's sending bombs over the backdrop. One is sailing over the edge at present, Sir. Take cover, men!"

"Won't you stop him? Won't you please be our general?" begged the captain.

"I'd love to!" said Luke. "Just let me get my things."

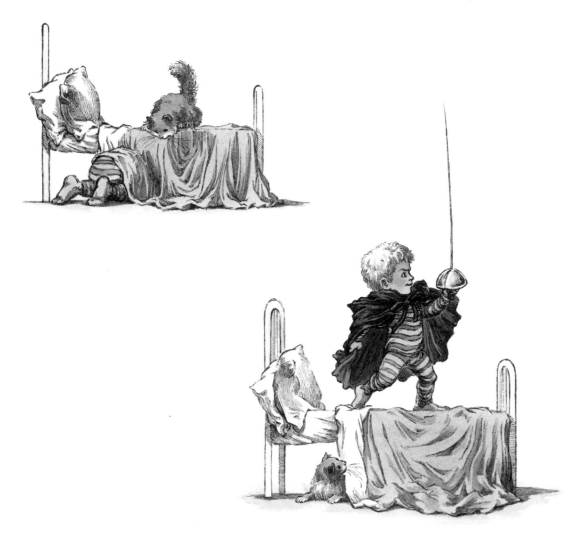

"He's through this doorway.
Stay here, men! We'll handle this!"
ordered Captain Fearsome.

"Maybe we could send him a letter of complaint instead," whispered the captain. "We could slowly turn around and —"

"Well, my dear Captain! And Luke—what are you doing out of bed, little boy?"

"Oh, I'm fainting!
Don't wake me up till he's gone!"

"Coward! You make my work easy!" snarled Longnose. "But I'll need stronger measures for the little one!"

17

"I won't miss again!" he spat.

"Yes! Run, little one, run!"

"Rags! We've got Longnose on the run!
Now's our chance—let's get him!"

"Yeow! Miserable cat!"

"It's all over, Longnose!"

"Tie him up, Captain, and take him to jail!"

"The fight's over, Rags," whispered Luke. "Let's go back to bed."

Luke was so tired that he hardly noticed
the theater beginning to shrink. "Goodnight, Luke!"
"Have pleasant dreams!" chanted everyone but Longnose . . .

Luke slept, quiet and content, the rest of the night.

McClintock, Barbara

The battle of Luke
and Longnose

$14.95

DATE